AN INCONVENIENT SÉANCE

A HESITANT MEDIUMS STORY

BELINDA KROLL

Bright
Bird Press

BRIGHT BIRD PRESS

This is a work of historical fantasy, and therefore a work of fiction. The appearance or mention of certain historical figures may be inevitable. Names, characters, organizations, places, events, and incidents are the product of the author's imagination or are used fictitiously. Any resemblance to actual events, locales, or persons, living or dead, is coincidental or historically-inspired. Eerie happenings during Victorian séances are to be expected, do try not to be too alarmed.

AN INCONVENIENT SÉANCE
A Hesitant Mediums short story
Copyright 2023 by Binaebi Akah Calkins
All rights reserved.

ISBN 978-1-7369213-5-7 (pb)
ISBN 978-1-7369213-4-0 (e)

Published by Bright Bird Press at prices that enable the creation of future works. Thank you for respecting the immense energy expended to create the work in your hands.

BELINDA KROLL

AN inconvenient SÉANCE

A HESITANT MEDIUMS STORY

Author Note

A Hesitant Mediums Story

"An Inconvenient Séance" is a short story between novels. This story is a standalone referencing characters and events from the historical fantasy romance novel, HAUNTING MISS TRENTWOOD, the first in the Hesitant Mediums series.

ONE

JUNE 1887, LONDON, ENGLAND

IN WHICH ONE ATTENDS A SEANCE

IT WAS A TRUTH universally acknowledged by all but Mrs. Steele that a séance was no place for matchmaking. With all the temerity of a woman desperate for grandchildren, Jasper Steele was unable to prevent his mother from calling upon her extensive network of friends, insisting they invite him to their popular séances.

For what better place might one stumble upon their future love than in a dark room dimly lit with romantic candles, holding hands and whispering secrets no one ought to know? And, with the Queen holding her own séances to reach her dearly departed Albert, this was practically a royally sanctioned method of matchmaking.

There really was nothing for it but to try.

As such, Jasper Steele found himself—after the incessant "encouragement" of his beloved mother—at his third séance for the week. While feeling much put upon, he was buoyed by the number of young ladies' hands he had indeed held thus far. And with the smiling endorsement of their mothers, no less.

The evening had started simply enough at the Carterprice household, with the usual cocktails and giggles, the rustling of bustled skirts and the hiss of lowered gas lamps. Under the watchful eyes of hopeful mothers, Jasper restrained himself to only a single glass of claret. He ran his fingers through his carefully coiffed blond hair, knowing the action made the tongue ladies sigh. He did well, hiding his amused smirk behind his mustache. He knew he cut a fine figure in his dark suit and gleaming shoes. While only a barrister's assistant, he delighted in a well-trimmed wardrobe.

Well-trained in how these evenings progressed, Jasper kept his replies to smiles and nods, allowing the young ladies to prattle on as though they were the center of his world. All the while he wondered if he might ever feel released from the wry observations of one Mary Trentwood, now happily engaged to his employer.

Mary never prattled.

It really was an annoying thing, witnessing their happiness while knowing it was Jasper's own fault for not recognizing Mary's charms soon enough.

Servants pulled velvet drapes shut against the London fog, turned down lamps to an intimate orange hue, and the gathering of some fifteen people dropped to wondering murmurs. Once again fighting what his mother termed his, "unwarranted doldrums over that girl," Jasper sat at a circular table. A winsome young brunette and her approving mother sat on either side of Jasper, clasping his hands with shy smiles.

Their hostess, Mrs. Carterprice, an imposing woman with an even more imposing bosom and stern features, nodded to her daughter to proceed. The séance began.

There were nervous giggles, and the circle shifted in anticipation. Jasper fought the urge to roll his eyes at Mrs. Carterprice's smug smile. He imagined what she might have put on the dinner menu, and who she might have placed him beside, for the young lady now gripping his hand, while not likely to prattle, also seemed unlikely to say anything at all. By Jove, he was so hungry and bored.

The young lady, who reminded him far too much of Mary, yanked Jasper from his morose reverie by digging her fingernails into his palm. He frowned at their clasped hands. This was exactly why he should have stayed home instead of indulging his mother. It was one thing to hold hands, tittering and whispering as the medium failed to retrieve a voice from the other side. It was entirely another thing to lose feeling in one's hand, and even worry about whether she might draw blood.

The gall exhibited by this crop of young ladies tonight was the definition of appalling.

"I beg your pardon," Jasper murmured, his blond mustache twitching as he fought to pull his hand from hers.

Her ash-white mother hissed, clawing the palm of his other hand.

He turned his attention to her, horrified. "Madam, you are untoward."

Jasper did not care if séances were the modern way to catch the eye of some young lady. No dowry, no promise of affection, was worth this abuse.

The young woman squeaked and nodded to the center of the round table at which they sat.

Jasper looked up to find a fetching young lady floating in the air, lifted by the waist like a rag doll. It was Miss Edith Carterprice, his childhood friend and their unfortunate medium for the evening. Her bustled skirts and flounced train dangled, exposing her shapely ankles. Now things were getting interesting. Jasper stared as convulsions threw Edith's blonde head back. Her arms hung, stiff at the elbows, her fingers twitching. She rotated in the air, a compass unsure which way was north, until stopping to face Jasper.

Her upside-down, unseeing stare sent chills down his back.

The brunette beside him whimpered.

Fortunately, or unfortunately, this was not Jasper's first haunting. He cleared his throat. "Dear Edith, I do believe you've lost your sense of gravity," he said, gratified to hear he sounded more cavalier than he felt.

The séance participants, already on edge, inhaled in unison.

Jasper blanched at the sight of Edith blinking one eye, then the other. He shifted in his seat, determined to break the summoning circle by grabbing Edith's shoulders and shaking her awake. This was, of course, right when the women on either side of him increased their grip such that he couldn't escape.

"Do not release his hand!" Mrs. Carterprice declared. "We don't know what might happen to Edith should we break the circle!"

Jasper glared at Mrs. Carterprice, hoping his thunderous expression showed he placed the blame for all of this on her head. Abominably perilous, hosting a séance without a proper medium, and terribly unfeeling to use her sensitive and quiet daughter as spiritual bait. Poor Edith had never enjoyed attention. As their mothers were friends, Jasper had always seen her, and her recently departed twin sister, as younger siblings to protect.

What on earth had made Edith agree to be a medium for her mother? Did she not know ghosts were real?

Jasper's most recent haunting escapade was but a couple of months ago, and he was still coming to terms with those ghostly encounters. He was not nearly ready for this singling out. His ego still stung from his panicked response at the countryside haunting.

What happens in the English countryside stays in the countryside, he kept telling himself. He straightened his shoulders and nodded. It was clear the spirit world had more to ask of him.

"Right then," Jasper snapped. "Let's have it out, shall we?"

Edith's soft blonde locks fell from her carefully piled chignon, sweeping the table as she hovered. "Jasper Ssssteele," she said in a deep, echoing voice, "you must help her."

Mrs. Carterprice nodded to Jasper, encouraging him to engage. The room fell silent, anticipation charging the air.

Jasper cleared his throat, feeling as though he had swallowed cotton. "Help whom?"

Edith blinked, her expression clearing, hinting at her horror behind the possession. "My sister," she whispered. With a quiet gasp, she crashed to the table. When she did not move, the séance participants leaned forward, unsure whether she breathed.

Jasper frowned. Now this wouldn't do. "Your sister?"

Edith rolled to her side, blinking. "Eloise, you mustn't," she whispered before fainting.

Jasper met the concerned gaze of Mrs. Carterprice with one of his own. The infamous Eloise Carterprice, Edith's twin, had died in a carriage accident not six months prior.

While Edith remained unconscious, a white, translucent fog emanated from her body. The fog took her shape, looking more and more like Edith curled on the table, docile as a sleeping kitten. The fog was Edith, yet not. Edith sighed in her sleep, whereas the translucent vision raised her head and stretched her arms. Dressed in a pale lavender, Eloise locked her whited-over eyes on Jasper.

"Eloise?" he breathed. He recoiled from the way her pupils, glazed over with a glossy whitewash, widened at the sight of him.

The ghostly Eloise scrambled across the table, kicking aside her skirts. She ignored the outraged gasps, not caring that she crawled through her sister Edith to reach Jasper, who sat appalled and terrified and annoyed that he was once again interacting with ghosts.

He really needed to find new acquaintances.

"Jasper, you'll help me. I know you will!" Eloise said. She swooped down, kissing him before he thought to duck.

He felt his face go rigid. Eloise caught his breath with her ghostly lips, feather-light and frozen. He could do nothing more than grunt his panic as his lungs burned. He lifted from the chair, his arms straining from the women still clutching him, holding him down from Eloise's strength. His face lost feeling. He kicked with wild abandon, hoping to leverage the table and throw himself away from Eloise.

When nothing worked, Jasper looked through Eloise to Mrs. Carterprice across the table. Mrs. Carterprice had the nerve to glare at him as if he had encouraged this otherworldly seduction.

"Eloise, that's enough," Mrs. Carterprice snapped.

Eloise dropped Jasper. "As ever, Mama, you're frightfully no fun."

Dazed and sprawled across the table beside the still-sleeping Edith, Jasper blinked up at Eloise's jubilant smile as a deep, distinctly male chuckle echoed around them.

Finally, screams filled the room.

TWO

IN WHICH ONE WAKES A GHOST

WHILE LIVING, ELOISE HAD always been ready for a laugh, especially if the laugh came with the misfortune of others. Yet even she had been rather put out upon waking with the odd realization that she was dead. And though she now felt compelled to be as amusing a nuisance as possible to her darling Jasper—really, how had she never noticed how brightly blue his eyes were, or how his sun-kissed blond hair flopped in the most flirtatious manner across his brow when disheveled—she also couldn't remember ever paying him much attention when alive.

Eloise had regarded Jasper Steele as rather a pompous, annoying twig of a boy, wasting his time rowing and telling her to stop doing what she wanted, and why couldn't she be more like her sedate sister, Edith.

So that certainly made for one of Eloise's many questions on why, and how, and for how long, she might be a ghost determinedly attached to one Jasper Steele. It wasn't her choice to be attached to him, and being so new at this ghostly experience, she hadn't any idea how to break free of him to have some real fun.

Leave it to boring sister Edith to call her back from Beyond and shackle her with the one man in whom Eloise hadn't any interest. And in a ghostly form as well!

Eloise soon realized being a ghost had odd restrictions. She couldn't taste the bonbons strewn across the side tables. They did go into her mouth, as it were, and crumble into pieces onto the floor as if her incorporeal teeth chewed them. Highly unsatisfying.

It also seemed once the séance circle broke apart, no one but Jasper could see her. As a woman known for (and delighted in) being noticed, this was beyond the pale.

Eloise decided her invisibility explained why everyone kept running *through* her; very rude. The action caused a peculiar, uncomfortable popping feeling in her joints. Rude and painful.

In the mirror over the fireplace, Eloise saw her own blue eyes glazed over with a cloudy white. Interestingly, she wore her favorite lavender gown rather than the fashionably frilly shroud from her funeral, and her hair styled in the best coiffure her French maid had ever crafted. It was as if she remained frozen in her state of dress upon death. Thank goodness she had died during her elopement.

Jasper, still sprawled on the table and watching Eloise's antics through wide eyes, reached over to shake Edith's shoulder.

Edith moaned as she roused, sleepily feeling for her missing glasses. At the sight of Jasper laying beside her, she gasped and fell back, almost off the table entirely, much to Elois's entertainment.

"Awake are we, sister dear?" Eloise said.

Edith, squinting in her ghostly sister's direction, felt for her glasses on her tinkling chatelaine amongst the folds of her overskirt. 'It can't be, it's never worked like that before," she kept murmuring.

Eloise smirked. "Mother made you take those ugly things off before the séance, you ninny."

Jasper climbed off the table, having regained his legs after Eloise had so smartly dropped him. He brushed invisible wrinkles from his waistcoat and smart pants, studiously avoiding the twins.

Rubbing her head, Edith glared at Eloise as she inched off the table, ignoring Jasper's solicitous hand. "Eloise, don't you know you're supposed to *leave* after the séance circle breaks?"

"When has your sister ever listened to rules?" their mother snipped from the drawing room doorway.

Eloise continued floating about the room, testing her abilities. "Jasper-poo," she said, "would you be a dear and hand me that wine?"

Jasper rolled his eyes. "Well, it's definitely Eloise," he muttered. "I hate that name."

Eloise floated over to his shoulder, watching with interest as he placed the glass in her hand. They both felt a spark, and Jasper jumped back.

Horror of horrors! Eloise couldn't taste the abandoned wine from the panicked séance guests streaming from her mother's house. Though, she could smash them against the walls in her frustration.

"That was an excellent claret," Jasper said.

"What is the point of coming back if I can't enjoy anything anymore?" Eloise wailed.

Edith, having found her glasses, situated them on her nose. "Indeed, why come back at all? I certainly didn't call for you."

Jasper backed away toward the door. Eloise felt a tug at the back of her neck, as though leashed. With a startled cry, she flew, not of her own accord, to Jasper's side.

Edith's mouth sagged open. "Eloise, you can't be serious."

"Serious?" Eloise snapped. "I've never been serious in my life, how dare you."

Jasper inched into the hallway. Eloise fought against the feeling of the tide dragging her heavy skirts out to sea. She squeezed her eyes shut. When Eloise opened them again, she popped into view beside Jasper, who stood open-mouthed, halfway out of the house with his hat in hand.

"Seems we're truly affianced," Eloise sang, pecking his cheek with her frostbitten lips.

"Not on your life, Eloise," Jasper ground out, "or your death, for that matter!"

Thus began Eloise's hours of pestering Jasper, for she had nothing better to do, and had no method to release her unexplained tether to Jasper. She hung off his shoulders as he ran from her former home along with the other guests, confirming no one else on the London streets was able to see her, either. Eloise complained about the unfashionable dinner plate his mother had saved for Jasper. She spun around him, begging to go dancing and wouldn't he drink just a little bit of wine to see if she might experience it through him and . . .

After entertaining herself until Jasper literally placed a pillow over his head to fall asleep, Eloise encountered another unexpected development. Upon his falling asleep, she no longer felt . . . leashed.

That seemed to be the only word worth using to describe the pull that kept Eloise close to Jasper. Instead, she found herself flitting around London all night, dragged by some unseen force until finally she found herself in an unfamiliar drawing room filled with familiar guests.

Her mother and twin sister were present, along with the indomitable Dame Hartwell holding court in her drawing room. They wore new clothes, and suddenly Eloise realized it must be morning. How interesting, she didn't seem to register hours of the day anymore. And why would she, when she was now immortal?

At least, that's what she had decided to call her ghostly experience. For surely having returned from the dead was as good as immortality?

It was an early morning tea, an odd time to hold another séance. And rude! Had they not just called her from Beyond last night, and now here they were calling more spirits forth so soon? Did they not care where she had disappeared to after the house cleared? Did they not wonder why she had left with Jasper Steele of all people, rather than stay to haunt the family?

Grumbling, Eloise floated in the corner, sensing a change in the air. She studied the expressions of these eager women pretending to enjoy their tea. They were waiting for something to occur, though she hadn't any idea what that might be.

When the quiet brunette sitting in the chair beside Dame Hartwell gently fell back, her cheek resting on the sloping wings of the high back, the room held its breath.

Eyes closed, the woman seemed asleep. She had dark circles under her eyes and sallow cheeks. Eloise floated closer and realized she was looking at none other than that timid mouse she knew from her season years ago, Mary Trentwood.

And really, how she had managed to return to London with Alexander Hartwell as her fiancé, having disappeared to her tiny little country house to take care of her ailing father, was beyond Eloise. And insulting, too, for Eloise had once tried to nab Hartwell for herself, before settling upon her own dear Rupert, rest his soul. She ought to find out whether Rupert was also a ghost, or if he made it to Beyond.

One never knew with Rupert. He had quite the reputation. There was a chance the Beyond hadn't accepted him.

Eloise would have shivered if she weren't a ghost.

Mary's chest rolled forward, her neck and head following slowly behind. At least, that's how it looked to everyone else.

To Eloise, she saw with much delight how the ghost of a saucy little parlor maid winked and sat down on Mary's lap. The effect was immediate. As the maid disappeared from view, Mary's body sat upright again.

Mary's eyes opened, and she said, "Oi, are those biscuits for just anyone?" She leaned forward, grabbed three cookies, and shoved them in her mouth. She chewed noisily, crumbs dusting Mary's fashionable lavender flounced overskirt.

"And who might you be, my dear?" Dame Hartwell said, her bright eyes snapping and her silver hair gleaming.

Possessed Mary shook her head. "Oh I'll not be saying anything about meself, not when you might send me Beyond!"

"Does one require a name to send one Beyond?" Dame Hartwell inquired.

"One might do well to refill me cup," the parlor maid's ghost quipped, waving Mary's tea cup at the dame.

The room leaned forward as one, with eyes bright and questions aplenty. Only Edith, Eloise's staid, demure, bespectacled sister, bothered to look in a different direction. In Eloise's direction, in fact.

"Don't look at me like that," Eloise snapped at her sister. "I didn't do anything to make that happen."

Edith blinked, turning an unbecoming green color.

"Oh for heaven's sake, Edith, you're acting like you've never seen a ghost before." Eloise floated over to her sister, sneering at the hand Edith held out in warning.

Before Eloise could say anything more, a peculiar feeling came over her, and the world faded to darkness.

THREE

IN WHICH ONE RECEIVES A WARNING

MARY TRENTWOOD STARTLED AWAKE in a cold sweat. She pawed at her high neckline, wishing she could undo a button for quick relief.

"Another sleepless night, my dear?" asked Dame Hartwell, her future mother-in-law. Her ice-blue eyes were bright with interest; indeed, her entire expression seemed absolutely delighted. She turned to her guests with a polite smile that belied her excitement. "As you can see, my daughter-in-law—well, soon-to-be—has had the most awful dreams since returning to London. I do think the Marylebone Spiritualist Association would be most interested in her case, don't you think?"

Mary caught her breath. She had done it again. She groaned inwardly, accepting a cup of lukewarm tea from the dame, cheeks aflame. She avoided the curious gazes of their guests. How mortifying, to have fallen asleep amongst such company.

"Fascinating," cried Mrs. Carterprice, the most fervent spiritualist of the lot. The mountain of lace atop her bosom jiggled with her excitement. "You truly do not know what has occurred?"

Mary froze, the teacup not quite to her lips. "Whatever do you mean?"

"Surely she jests," said another of the ladies. "It is a trick, the dame has cajoled her son's fiancée to play a trick on us."

Mary eyed the tea in her cup as her stomach churned. Dame Hartwell was far more sly than Mary gave her credit for. To be fair, the tea had tasted a little bitter, more than usual, yet nothing to remark about. It had a soothing effect on her nerves, a feeling Mary had appreciated given her recent insomnia. She should have guarded against it. It was in moments of restful calm that Mary heard the voices.

Dame Hartwell patted Mary's hand, now clenched around her teacup. "Our dear Mary has not yet learned the importance of her Sense. Her father, you know . . ." She let her voice trail off amid the knowing nods of her spiritualist compatriots.

Mary placed her teacup on its saucer as an excuse to pull away from Dame Hartwell. "I don't speak of my father," she murmured.

"Yes, yes, but we cannot understand why," Mrs. Carterprice said, impatient. "You've spoken with the other side! Surely you see how we cannot abandon you."

"Indeed," Mrs. Neal agreed. "If only the queen knew!"

Ah yes. The queen. In Queen Victoria's ever-present mourning over her beloved Prince Albert, word had gotten out that she hosted secret séances . . . and the gentry were unlikely to miss out on an entertaining trend that might engender an invitation from the queen.

Dame Hartwell was determined to make good on Mary's own harrowing experience to secure her place amongst the spiritualist ladies of her social class. Mary shuddered, still unable to shake the sight of her father's spirit crawling from his fresh grave. Did all spirits reach their clairvoyant charges in such a gruesome manner?

Dame Hartwell leaned back in her seat, seeming quite satisfied with herself. "We shall help our dear Mary overcome her shyness, shan't we, ladies?"

Mary resisted the urge to bolt from the room. She glanced at the clock, hoping the visiting hour would soon end. "I am not shy," she said, her voice growing firm. "I simply have no need to speak with ghosts, or let them speak through me. I prefer to keep my mind to myself."

"And what is the fun in that, when one might use the spirits to speak what we all wish to say anyway?" Mrs. Carterprice scoffed.

The front door crashed open, a sure sign that Alexander Hartwell, the dame's son and Mary's betrothed, had returned. Dame Hartwell's friends tittered at the obvious way Mary perked to attention.

"We should have guessed she had lost interest, with her fiancé due to return," they whispered to one another.

Mary stared at the doorway, willing Hartwell to poke his head into view and silence the women surrounding her.

"Hullo!" Hartwell said, striding into the parlor. He bent to kiss his mother's cheek, and turned to take Mary's hand in his own. "And what have we here, Mother? Why does Mary look so drawn?"

"I am looking like no such thing," Mary protested.

Eyebrows rose at Mary contradicting him. One hardly did such things. But then, one hardly spoke with ghosts, either.

Hartwell grinned and gave Mary a quick peck on the cheek. "You are looking drawn, and I can guess the cause." He rounded on the ladies. "I fear I must beg pardon. I simply must steal my betrothed and insist she rest."

Despite the scar that sliced his face from temple to cheek, Hartwell had a charm which won over the crustiest of people. All smiles and laughter, that was Mary's Hartwell. It was an endearing quality, and one Mary wished she could exhibit herself.

With a little scowl, Dame Hartwell bid her friends farewell, shooing them from the house with promises of another time.

As soon as the last lady's skirts swished from the house, Hartwell pointed at his mother. "You tricked me. You tricked us," he said, far too calm.

Dame Hartwell waved him away. "It does you no good or credit to be worrying after Mary so. You know if she does not release this tension with her Sense—"

"Dame Hartwell," Mary interrupted, "I can handle my situation. I only wish you would not use me for sport with your friends."

Hartwell scowled. "Mother, if you insist on making Mary your parlor trick, I shall have to insist on always being in attendance."

Dame Hartwell pouted. "But you would only put a stop to it, if you were here."

"Just so," he replied.

Mary rubbed her forehead, trying to forget what she saw in her trance. She could only tell falsehoods to these women for so long before they found her out. Usually, after chatting with some spirit that wandered into view, Mary's persistent headache dissipated for a blessed couple of days. Not so this time. No, this time, her headache increased in pressure.

Sharp needles stung behind Mary's eyes. She pressed the heels of her hands against her temples.

"What is it?" Hartwell dropped to his knee before her. "Shall I ring for Pomeroy?"

Mary's head snapped up. She felt compelled to look to the fireplace, empty of fire in the early summer heat. How had she not noticed the young woman who remained behind the others? She glanced at Hartwell, her expression crestfallen.

Hartwell stood and placed his hand on her shoulder in silent comfort. He looked about the room, his unseeing eyes confirming the worst for Mary.

"Alex," Mary whispered, staring at the slight woman in horrified embarrassment, "we are not alone."

Dame Hartwell clapped with delight. "Who do you see?" she breathed.

Mary shook her head, unsure if she should speak or encourage the woman to speak.

The ghost was about Mary's age, lit as if a fire burned beside her. Her lavender dress was a pretty, frilly thing, complete with the latest style in bustle and train. She piled her blonde hair atop her head in the latest fashion, complete with fringed bangs. Her dark eyes bore into Mary. She looked familiar, appallingly so. But who would Mary know in London so recently dead?

Mary's head tilted. She thought of the quiet blonde woman who had hid behind her glasses beside Mrs. Carterprice during tea. Mary knew her as Edith, and both she and her mother had worn full mourning for a sister recently deceased amidst a scandal. This ghost was Edith Carterprice's mirror image. Mary's mouth sagged open.

The ghost, who Mary suspected was the infamous Eloise Carterprice, held up her hand for silence. "I'm bade to tell you," her voice hollow and echoing, "that danger arrives." With that, she turned and disappeared into the wall.

FOUR

IN WHICH ONE SEEKS REFUGE

JASPER SPENT MUCH OF the next day experimenting with ways to rid himself of Eloise. Burning incense only made her pretend to sneeze, or at least Jasper assumed she was pretending, for whoever heard of a ghost with a sensitive nose? Besides, their housekeeper came in, very disapproving, and snuffed it out with her bare fingertips with a decidedly stern expression.

"Was she your nanny, Jasper-poo?" Eloise asked, amused and impressed.

He ignored Eloise, shoving his arms into his coat sleeves and tying his cravat most haphazardly.

"Are we going somewhere?" Eloise asked, hovering behind him in the mirror.

Jasper yelped at the sight of her white eyes and bluish lips. No matter, he didn't need to see what he was doing to finish his dress. He strode from his bedroom with the speed of a man chased by the devil, for indeed he was. Eloise floated behind him at a leisurely pace, as if one might pace while floating. Jasper slapped his short top hat to his head and escaped before his mother might notice.

He loved his mother dearly, but this was hardly the time for her interest now that he not only had a ghost thinking she was his fiance, but he also had an actual date to keep with a young lady and her mother.

By the time Jasper had walked the distance across the Paddington Street Garden to the charming little tea shop, he suspected Eloise had realized his intent. She was too clever by half and chose not to say a word until Jasper hailed the young lady and her mother. They sat where they might see and be seen.

"Oh Jasper, certainly you can do better than this," Eloise murmured in his ear as he removed his hat to sit down.

He waved his hat as if a gnat annoyed him. "Terribly sorry for my lateness. I'd have arrived sooner, but there was a to-do this morning."

The mother, for in Jasper's hasty acceptance, he had entirely forgotten their names, assessed him with a raised brow. He winced, knowing he must look a sight.

"I do hope everything has resolved by now?" the mother asked.

"Will you need to return? I would hate to keep you from something important," the daughter whispered.

Jasper leaned forward, frowning, almost unable to catch what she had said. Really. What was her name? He resolved to stop letting his mother schedule his dates. He couldn't imagine having dinner with someone every night who wouldn't put forth the effort to speak louder than a whisper.

"She asked whether you want to stay for this pathetic date or if she might go back to her books," Eloise sneered. She sat on the edge of the table, picking at her fingernails as if removing dirt from beneath them.

Upon further studying, Jasper realized Eloise did, in fact, have dirt under her fingernails. And if he focused, she looked… damp. He remembers the papers saying she had drowned. The exciting conclusion to her failed elopement and crashed carriage escapade.

Clearing his throat, Jasper assured, "Nothing for you to worry about. I wouldn't have missed our meeting for the world."

Eloise rolled her eyes with a snort. "You ought to have. You look awful. Shadows under your eyes, you didn't comb your hair, and your cravat! You look as though you rolled out of your mistress's bed." She leaned forward. "Do you have a mistress, Jasper-poo? Should I haunt you during your assignations?"

Jasper choked on his sip of tea, glaring at Eloise.

The mother and daughter shared a bewildered look.

"How is your dear mother?" Mrs. Bennington asked, for Jasper had just remembered her name. She wore a black silk gown with all the proper flounces and layers, and a high neck with buttons running the full length of the dress. She had a perched little hat, as was the fashion, and she looked quite smart, especially with her salt-and-pepper hair.

In contrast, Miss Bennington wore an unbecoming brown thing without adornments that barely fit her body. It pinched in the wrong places and even sagged in others. Her hair was dark and swept up into a long, thick braid coiled into a bun at the top of her neck, and her hat, the most attractive thing about her, showcased a little blue bird sitting at a jaunty angle.

"Mother is delighted we are finally meeting," Jasper said. He eyed Eloise, who was lifting a sugar cube with the little silver tongs. He grabbed them before the Benningtons might notice.

"Oh," Miss Bennington said, a little frown creasing her brow, "did you want another sugar? I am dreadfully sorry. I ought to have asked."

Jasper shook his head with a tight smile, trying not to appear as if he fought for control over the tongs. "No indeed, I was simply admiring the craft work of this instrument. My mother would love a pair."

Eloise cackled, releasing the tongs so abruptly they went flying into a cup on the table beside them with a satisfying splash.

Jasper pressed his lips together, resisting the urge to wipe his hand down his face.

It was now Mrs. Bennington's turn to clear her throat as she gathered her purse from her lap, nodding to her daughter. "Well, Mr. Steele," she said with decisive tones. "This has been educational."

Miss Bennington stood with her mother, her eyes wide. Jasper knew the look. She couldn't believe her mother was saying no to a suitor, in the same way his mother wouldn't believe he had chased away another potential bride.

"It's been charming," Jasper said, defeated.

"Do send our regards to your poor–that is, dear–to your mother?" Mrs. Bennington said, taking her daughter's arm as they backed away.

Jasper nodded, waving them away with a half-resigned, half-dismissive attitude. He watched as they practically stumbled from the tea shop and hailed a cab while looking over their shoulders as though afraid of being chased.

They were right to be cautious.

Eloise plucked Mrs. Bennington's purse from her wrist and dropped it into the mud just as the hackney rolled into place. She held the door shut, so that when Miss Bennington tugged harder to open it, she smacked her mother in the face as she returned to standing after retrieving her purse. She then slammed the door shut behind them, shouting something about leaving her Jasper-poo alone as they rolled into traffic.

Jasper, giving up any pretense of sanity, put his forehead to the table with a low groan.

"Sir?"

Jasper rolled his head to the side, his cheek resting on the tablecloth. He peered at the waiter standing beside him with a pinched expression.

"I don't suppose you intend to settle the cheque?"

The following morning, Jasper sat at his mother's breakfast table, positively wilted. Though his mother required all the niceties of dress as if they had guests, he could not put the energy into changing out of his clothes from the night before. He stripped off his jacket and rolled up his shirtsleeves, and his waistcoat flapping open as he slouched. Jasper looked a rumpled mess, and quite twitchy, too.

Mrs. Steele's narrow green eyes observed Jasper over her teacup rim as she sipped. Her thin, white fingers gripped the teacup as Jasper's attention darted about the room. He had taken to doing that since returning home from his visit to Compton Beauchamp. While Jasper had kept to himself the most alarming details of everything that had occurred at Gideon Trentwood's house in that little back-of-beyond village, he was unable to prevent his mother witnessing him changed, and harmed, and skittish.

"I take it that the evening's events did not go as we hoped?" she ventured after another deep sigh escaped Jasper.

"Not hardly," he snorted. He sat up, glaring at his father's seat at the head of the table.

His mother followed his gaze. Jasper could tell by her frown that she was unable to see Eloise Carterprice perched atop her husband's seat with all the regal censure of the queen herself. "My dear, why do you stare at your father's seat?"

Eloise grinned at Jasper, daring him to tell the truth.

"No reason," he ground out, running his hand down his face. "It was a rough night, Mother, and my eyes betray me."

"You had a rough night," Eloise said, catching a laugh. "How do you think I feel? Watching you ignore me all night, though we both know you can't unsee me. We've kissed, Jasper darling, don't you think that means something? Surely things haven't changed so much since my passing that you can ignore such a thing between a man and a woman!"

Jasper angled his head away from Eloise, trying to block out her grating voice without alarming his mother further.

So it had gone the entire night with Eloise pestering him, refusing to allow him to sleep. It wasn't just that he hadn't the energy to undress—it was that she had insisted upon hovering about, commenting on every little thing. He could hardly change into his nightshirt with her there in the corner, arms crossed over her ample bosom, a knowing smirk causing his blood to freeze.

If Eloise thought a mere kiss doomed him to her constant presence, just what did she think seeing him *naked* meant?

"I am sorry to hear it," Mrs. Steele said. "You know I only hope for the best for you, my dear, and I do worry so after your return from Compton Beauchamp. Your head . . ."

Jasper touched the side of his head, self-conscious. He had taken to growing his hair out rather longer these days, in the style of the poets, to hide the bump that would not entirely heal. Another artifact from the summer's ghostly events that he'd rather not remember. "My head is fine, Mother."

"Is it?" Mrs. Steele asked, her piqued tone revealing her annoyance.

"Indeed, is it?" Eloise echoed, her tinkling laugh razing over Jasper's nerves.

Downing his tea in a single gulp, Jasper grabbed a slice of toast and stood from the table.

"Jasper!" Mrs. Steele said. "Whatever are you doing?"

"I'm off to the Hartwell house, I think," he said before jamming the toast in his mouth.

Eloise eyed him, suspicious. "She can't help you," she warned.

"Why? Why must you continue to torture yourself with being in the presence of that woman?" Mrs. Steele muttered. "Is it not enough that she rejected you?"

Jasper paused, seeing how small and unhappy his mother looked. He sighed, leaning to kiss her forehead. "I don't visit with the Hartwells to torture myself, Mother. There are some things one experiences that require certain company, because they know and understand."

"Who could possibly understand you more than your mother?" Mrs. Steele said.

"Mary Trentwood saved me, Mother, and I do think she might do it again." Jasper spun on his heel, a glint in his eye as he stalked past Eloise, who now hovered by the doorway, mouth agape.

"The Trentwood girl!" Eloise breathed, trailing behind him like the wretched wraith she was as he practically ran from the house and down the street. "The ghosts won't stop talking about her, are you going to visit her?"

"Visit her?" Jasper barked. "I'm going to beg her to exorcize you."

Eloise giggled. "Well, she can't do that, not in her state."

Jasper stuttered to a halt. Had Eloise been corporeal, they surely would have toppled to the ground. Instead, he suffered the unfortunate, nauseating chill of her body sliding through his.

"What's wrong with Mary? I just saw her the other day. She seemed . . . quite well."

"As well as one could be, for a woman who's doing her best to dampen a rather heightened Sense." Eloise leaned forward, once again taking advantage of her ghostly form to be entirely too forward, and in public, too.

"Sense?"

Eloise waved her hand. "You know, her ability to commune with the spirits and Beyond. Surely you knew this, you pursued her, didn't you?"

Jasper colored.

Tsking with a grin, Eloise ran a finger down Jasper's waistcoat. Her slow smile revealed her pleasure at his uncomfortable shiver. "Mary Trentwood is more likely to immolate herself with her unused powers than she is to do any good with them."

"Immolate?" Jasper swallowed. "Surely you're being dramatic."

"Oh no," Eloise said archly. "It's all the gossip amongst us spirits. Miss Trentwood's a flickering beacon, gathering ghosts about her as moths to a flame. Those spirits will smother her if she doesn't control her Sense." She rubbed her hands together. "You know, when a medium burns out, it's actually quite delicious. Such a dispelling can maintain a spirit for decades, I'm told."

"Eloise," Jasper breathed, spinning on his heel, "you are the absolute worst."

"I am, am I not?" Eloise floated alongside him with a self-satisfied chortle, clearly keeping additional details to herself in a successful effort at frustrating him further.

Jasper shoved his hands into his pockets and strode on, his mind racing. Just what did he think poor Mary Trentwood could do for him, if indeed she couldn't help herself? Jasper adjusted the brim of his hat to hide his stormy expression from passersby, his mood worsening as he reconciled the thought that they were once again hurtling toward another ghostly adventure.

*Read Jasper's complete story in the next installment of the Hesitant Mediums series: **A Spirited Engagement***

Message from the Author

I hope you had as much fun reading this as I had writing it.
If you liked this book, please consider writing a review at one
of the locations below. As an independent author, your reviews
and word-of-mouth are key to the success of this book and my
writing career.

Website https://worderella.com
BookBub https://worderella.com/bookbub
Goodreads https://worderella.com/goodreads

Become a VIP

If you would like to be contacted when I release a new work, subscribe to my newsletter or become a patron of my community, the Cozy Coterie. Cozy Coterie patrons receive discounts from my store, including exclusive editions.

Newsletter https://worderella.com/vip
Cozy Coterie https://worderella.com/cozycoterie

Titles by Belinda Kroll

HESITANT MEDIUMS

Haunting Miss Trentwood
Miss Preston's Predicament (story)
An Inconvenient Séance (story)
A Spirited Engagement

OTHER TITLES

The Last April
Catching the Rose

Beatrice Learns to Dance
as Binaebi Akah

Haunting Miss Trentwood

Book 1 of the Hesitant Mediums

It is a truth universally acknowledged that father knows best, even after death, and especially about one's suitors.

Resigned to spinsterhood in her English manor house, Mary Trentwood is horrified when her father's ghost crawls from his grave, and struggles as he spouts opinion after opinion about the *most mundane* things.

Mistaking the newly-arrived and quietly handsome Alexander Hartwell as her father's solicitor—for who else would interrupt her mourning?—Mary soon realizes her father is adding matchmaking to his repertoire. Neither Mary nor her father realize Hartwell hunts a blackmailer, and shouldn't waste time seeking Mary's smiles…

Miss Preston's Predicament
A Hesitant Mediums story

*It is a truth universally ignored, most principally by the dowager
Dame Hartwell, that ghosts and gatherings do not mix.*

In this short story, the fashionable and eccentric dowager Dame
Hartwell has lured the reclusive Miss Tessa Preston to attend her
drawing room séance. If Dame Hartwell can't convince Miss
Preston, her former protégé, to return as her medium-in-res-
idence, she doesn't know how she will protect her son and
his new fiancée from the brewing storm of malcontent spirits
surrounding them.

MISS PRESTON'S PREDICAMENT is a short story be-
tween novels. It is a standalone referencing characters and events
from the cozy Victorian fantasy romance, HAUNTING MISS
TRENTWOOD, the first in the Hesitant Mediums series.

An Inconvenient Séance

A Hesitant Mediums story

It is a truth universally ignored that sons abhor being sent to séances in search of a wife.

In this short story, Jasper Steele has had enough of ghosts to last him a lifetime, so why is he attending a séance? Mostly to appease his mother, who worries about his head and his heart after his summer in the English countryside getting rejected by Mary Trentwood.

Eloise Carterprice has never been one to let a good opportunity escape her, so it's only natural that her ghost appears during the latest séance hosted by her mother. Will Jasper find a bit of romance? Will Eloise have her bit of fun? Read on, dear Reader, read on!

This is a short story bridge between HAUNTING MISS TRENTWOOD and A SPIRITED ENGAGEMENT. It is a companion story to "Miss Preston's Predicament."

A SPIRITED ENGAGEMENT
BOOK 2 OF THE HESITANT MEDIUMS

It is a truth universally acknowledged that ghost brides are annoying romantic rivals.

Making her reluctant return to London after a ten-year absence, Tessa Preston cannot hide her dismay at her employer's friendliness with Jasper Steele, the man who chased her away. To make matters more annoying, he's haunted by a *most insistent* ghost bride.

Determined to prove her indifference to the charming Jasper, Tessa realizes the entitled ghost demanding his attention may not be all she seems. Meanwhile, unaware of Tessa's enmity, Jasper is delighted to have a second chance at her affections, and will let nothing, not even her cold stares, dampen his enthusiasm.

A SPIRITED ENGAGEMENT is a standalone romantic fantasy featuring characters from the cozy Victorian fantasy romance, HAUNTING MISS TRENTWOOD, the first in the Hesitant Mediums series.

About the Author

Belinda Kroll writes sweet and cozy Victorian romantasy, where Jane Austen vocabulary meets modern sass. She is a user experience design professional, hobbyist photographer, and lindy hopper.

Kroll is obsessed with eyeglasses, Korean dramas, home renovation and cooking shows, and petting every dog that allows her to do so. She has a line of stationery for writers, readers, and creatives at Bright Bird Press. She lives with her family in Ohio.

Website https://worderella.com
Instagram https://instagram.com/worderella
Membership https://worderella.com/cozycoterie
Bright Bird Press stationery https://brightbirdpress.com